For my Mia. I love
you so much!

Mia the mermaid
had a long day.

All day long she
played and played.

Mia and her
friends played
hide and seek.

Hide real fast
and don't make
a peep!

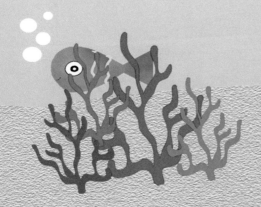

Next, they
searched for
jewels in the sand.
Look! Mia found
a jewel for
each hand.

They dressed up in
hats and played
catch with a ball.

Then had a tea
party, and played
with her doll.

But the day is gone,
and now it's night.

Time to turn
out every light.

"But there is so much to do!" Mia the mermaid said.

"So much to do before I go to bed."

First, she has to
brush her teeth,
back and forth,
and up and down.

Now it's time
for her
nightgown.

She feels like a
princess wearing her
night dress, and this
gown just has to
impress.

For the next step in
her bedtime routine is
very important, very
important indeed!

She has to bestow
a kiss, to a most
handsome prince.
It started when
she was a baby, and
it's been a tradition
ever since.

The prince is her
Daddy who
hugs her tight,
kisses her head,
and whispers
"Goodnight."

The End

Color Mia the Mermaid and her friends!

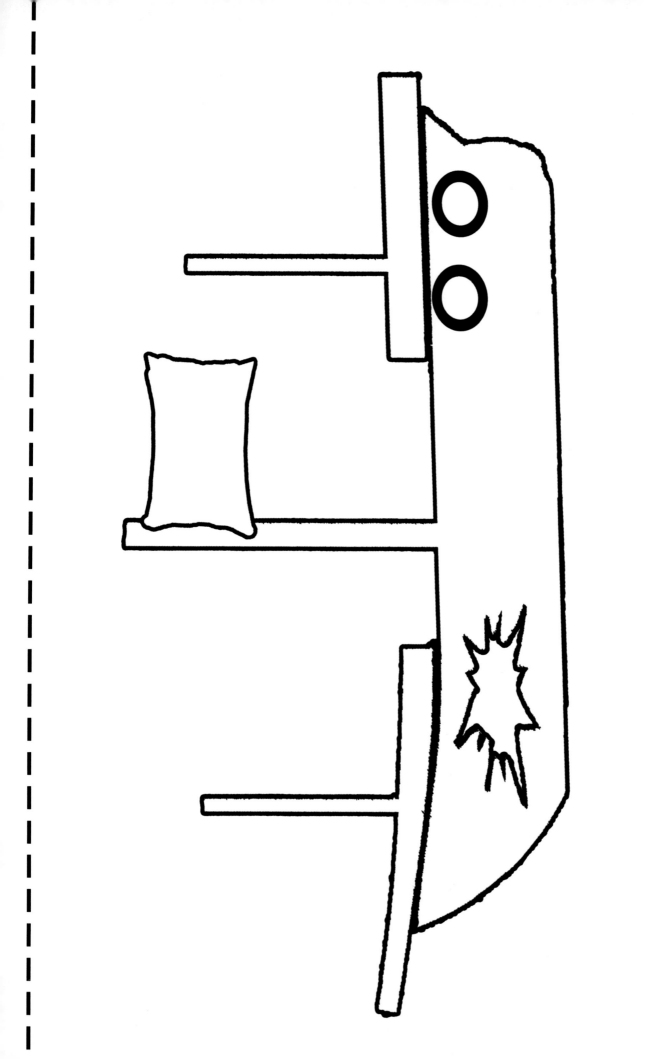

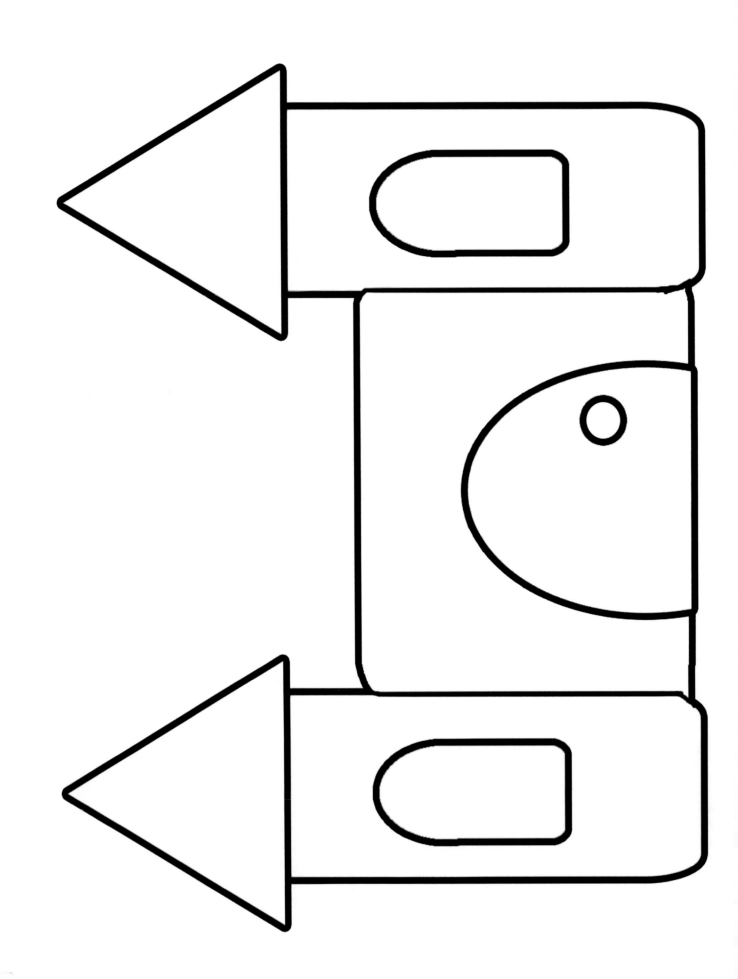

Made in the USA
Middletown, DE
30 November 2016